THE FREAKY FUNKY
FRENCH FRIES
RHYTHM AND RHYME

The A B C's

Kindergarten-Second Grade

Jonquil Steele

Dedicated to the most wonderful children in the world… Cortlynd, Jamiel, Parist and Landymn… love you all, Mom

ISBN 978-1-64299-828-3 (hardcover)
ISBN 978-1-64299-829-0 (digital)

Christian Faith Publishing, Inc.
832 Park Avenue
Meadville, PA 16335
www.christianfaithpublishing.com

Printed in the United States of America

Freaky Funky French Fry Pledge

I pledge allegiance to the grind
of the Freaky Funky French Fries
rhythm and rhyme
We'll be saying this pledge from time to time
to help you make your memory climb
The French Fries promise you will do just fine
so listen to the reader and repeat each line
This book is for our ABC's
it's gonna be
fun just wait and see

Come on everyone and practice this beat
loosen up and wiggle in your seat
by clapping your hands and stomping your feet

Left foot stomp
Right foot stomp
Clap your hands

Keep going with the
foot stomp foot stomp clap
while reading the book

And at the bottom of each
page are the vocabulary words
with pronunciation and syllable count

Aa

The soccer **<u>athlete</u>** flew
in the **<u>airplane</u>** to
get to the **<u>arena</u>**

<u>athlete</u> [ath-leet] 2 claps

<u>airplane</u> [air-pleyn] 2 claps

<u>arena</u> [uh-ree-nuh] 3 claps

athlete- {person good at games}
airplane- {aircraft with wings supported by air}
arena- {enclosed area used for public entertainment}

Come on everyone and practice this beat
loosen up and wiggle in your seat
by clapping your hands and stomping your feet
Left foot stomp
Right foot stomp
Clap your hands
Practice the beat three times

Bb

The **<u>baby</u>** was sleeping
and the **<u>brother</u>** saw
so he grabbed a **<u>blanket</u>**

<u>baby</u> [bey-bee] 2 claps

<u>brother</u> [bruhth-er] 2 claps

<u>blanket</u> [blang-kit] 2 claps

baby- {very young child}
brother- {male person related to you and
having same mother or father}
blanket- {covering used for beds}

Cc

We were playing at the
carnival and saw a **caramel**
colored camel

carnival [kahr-nuh-vuh l] 3 claps

caramel [kar-uh-muh l] 3 claps

colored [kuhl-erd] 2 claps

camel [kam-uh l] 2 claps

carnival- {entertainment that travels from town to town}
caramel- {burnt sugar used for coloring and flavoring}
color- {fill in the outlines of a shape or picture with color}
camel- {large hoofed animal that has one
or two large humps on its back}

Come on everyone and practice this beat
loosen up and wiggle in your seat
by clapping your hands and stomping your feet
Left foot stomp
Right foot stomp
Clap your hands
Practice the beat two times

Dd

Me and my **dad** were
at the **dance** and
we **danced** till **dusk**

dad [dad] 1 clap

dance [dahns] 1 clap

danced [dahns-d] 1 clap

dusk [duhsk] 1 clap

dad-{father}
dance- {gathering where people go, and music is played}
danced- {movements in time to music}
dusk- {time when the sky is getting dark at night}

Ee

We **<u>entered</u>** the gym to
<u>exercise</u> and we
all left **<u>exhausted</u>**

<u>entered</u> [en-ter-ed] 3 claps

<u>exercise</u> [ex-ser-sahyz] 3 claps

<u>exhausted</u> [ig-zawst-d] 3 claps

enter- {to come or go into}
exercise- {bodily activity}
exhausted- {to tire out}

Ff

While the **farmer** was
feeding the **flowers**
he saw a **feather**

farmer [fahr-mer] 2 claps

feeding [fee-din] 2 claps

flower [flou-er] 2 claps

feather [feth-er] 2 claps

farmer- {work or runs a farm}
feeding- {to give food to}
flower- {plant part that produces seeds}
feather- {coverings of a bird}

Gg

The **giant** grew a
bunch of **greens** so
he could **grow**

giant [jahy-uh nt] 2 claps

greens [greenz] 1 clap

grow [groh] 1 clap

giant- {person of great size and strength}
greens- {a leafy vegetable}
grow- {to spring upwards}

Hh

At **<u>home</u>** there was
<u>homework</u> that was very
<u>hard</u> and they only had
an **<u>hour</u>**

<u>home</u> [hohm] 1 clap

<u>homework</u> [hohm-wurk] 2 claps

<u>hard</u> [hahrd] 1 clap

<u>hour</u> [ou-er] 2 claps

home- {house or apartment where a person lives}
homework- {school lessons to be done at home}
hard{not easy}
hour- {a fixed time}

Ii

Invent and **imagine**
living in an **igloo**
castle surrounded
by **ice**

invent [in-vent] 2 claps

imagine [ih-maj-in] 3 claps

igloo [ig-loo] 2 claps

ice [ahys] 1 clap

invent- {to create for the first time}
imagine- {form a mental picture of}
igloo- {house made of blocks of snow}
ice- {frozen water}

Wiggle and jiggle up and down
place your hands on your hips
now stretch to the left
now stretch to the right

Jj

Jog to the **jewelers**
to get the **jade**
green **jewelry**

jewelers [joo-uh-lerz] 3 claps

jade [jeyd] 1 clap

jewelry [joo-uh l-ree] 3 claps

jeweler- {person who makes, buys, and sells jewelry}
jade- {green mineral}
jewelry- {rings or necklaces worn on the body}

Kk

The **kids** **keep** their
kite in the
kitchen

kids [kidz] 1 clap

keep [keep] 1 clap

kite [kahyt] 1 clap

kitchen [kich-uh n] 2 claps

kids-{child}
keep- {to put in a specified space for storage}
kite- {light covered frame for flying in the air}
kitchen- {a room in which cooking is done}

Ll

The **landing** strips **location**
was **located** by
the **lodge**

landing [lan-ding] 2 claps

location [loh-key-shuh n] 3 claps

located [loh-keyt-d] 3 claps

lodge [loj] 1 clap

landing- {a place for unloading passengers}
location- {a particular place}
locate- {to find the position of}
lodge- {temporary living or sleeping space}

Mm

Many people try
to **maintain**
a **magnet** school

many [men-ee] **2 claps**

maintain [meyn-teyn] **2 claps**

magnet [mag-nit] **2 claps**

many- {being one of a large but not definite number}
maintain- {to keep in a particular or desired state}
magnet- {a thing or person that attracts}

Nn

The **newcomer** felt
natural saying
nada

newcomer [noo-kuhm-er] 3 claps

natural [nach-er-uh l] 3 claps

nada [nah-duh] 2 claps

newcomer- {someone recently arrived}
natural- {being or acting as expected}
nada- {a Spanish word meaning nothing}

Oo

My **<u>objective</u>** for
today is to **<u>observe</u>** an
<u>ordinary</u> <u>occupation</u>

<u>objective</u> [uh b-jek-tiv] 3 claps

<u>observe</u> [uh b-zurv] 2 claps

<u>ordinary</u> [awr-dn-er ee] 4 claps

<u>occupation</u> [ok-yuh-pey-shuh n] 4 claps

objective- {purpose or goal}
observe- {to watch carefully}
ordinary- {normal or usual}
occupation- {a person's business or profession}

Are you loosened up
and feeling good ?
We the French Fries knew you would

Pp

The **postman** stacked
his **package**
on the **pallet**

postman [pohst-muh n] 2 claps

package [pak-ij] 2 claps

pallet [pal-it] 2 claps

postman- {letter carrier}
package- {bundle made up for mailing}
pallet- {low portable platform on which goods are placed}

Qq

The **queen** made
a **quilt** out of
four **quadrants**

queen [kween] 1 clap

quilt [kwilt] 1 clap

quadrants [kwod-ruh nts] 2 claps

queen- {woman who rules a country or kingdom}
quilt- {a bed cover made of cloth}
quadrant- {any four parts into which something is divided}

Kids are smart as Owls
and limber like trees
bend forward and touch your knees

Rr

Researchers have
to **reciprocate recipes**
for **root** beer

researchers [ree-surch-ers] **3 claps**

reciprocate [ri-sip-ruh-keyt] **4 claps**

recipes [res-uh-peez] **3 claps**

root [root] **1 clap**

researchers- {a person who investigates thoroughly}
reciprocate- {to give or feel in return}
recipe- {instructions for making something
by combining various things}
root- {leafless underground part of a plant}

Ss

A **<u>siegmeister</u>** held
his **<u>stance</u>** on
the **<u>scaffold</u>**

<u>siegmeister</u> [sig-mahy-ster] 3 claps

<u>stance</u> [stans] 1 clap

<u>scaffold</u> [skaf-uh ld] 2 claps

siegmeister- {composer}
stance- {position of the body while standing}
scaffold- {raised platform built for support}

Freaky Funky French Fry Pledge

I pledge allegiance to the grind
of the Freaky Funky French Fries
rhythm and rhyme
We'll be saying this pledge from time to time
to help you make your memory climb
The French Fries promise you will do just fine
so listen to the reader and repeat each line
This book is for our ABC's
it's gonna be
fun just wait and see

Tt

Ternary people fit
on the **teeterboard**
because it was
tempting

ternary [tur-nuh-ree] **3 claps**

teeterboard [tee-ter-bawrd] **3 claps**

tempting [temp-ting] **2 claps**

ternary- {three}
teeterboard- {a seesaw}
tempting- {to consider doing something wrong}

Uu

We **unveiled** the **ukulele**
from **underneath**
the **underarm**

unveiled [un-veiled] 2 claps

ukulele [uku-le-le] 3 claps

underneath [un-der-neath] 3 claps

underarm [un-der-arm] 3 claps

unveiled- {to show or make known to the public}
ukulele- {a small guitar with four strings}
underneath- {directly under}
underarm- {armpit}

Vv

The **viator** chose to
veer to the left so
he could get
some **venison**

viator [vahy-ey-tawr] 3 claps

veer [veer] 1 clap

venison [ven-uh-suh n] 3 claps

viator- {traveler}
veer- {to change direction}
venison- {the meat of a deer used for food}

Ww

Wangdoodle and **whoosis**
were **whigging**

wangdoodle [whang-doo-duhl] 3 claps

whoosis [hoo-zis] 2 claps

whigging [hwig-ging] 2 claps

wangdoodle- {something one doesn't know the name of}
whoosis- {an object or person whose name is not known}
whig- {to move along briskly}

Xx

xenia was flying around
xerarch causing
xerosis

xenia [zee-nee-uh] 3 claps

xerarch [zeer-ahrk] 2 claps

xerosis [zi-roh-sis] 3 claps

xenia-{pollen}
xerarch- {a dry habitat}
xerosis- {dry eyes or skin}